DORA
AND THE
UNICORN KING

adapted by Ellie Seiss
based on the screenplay "King Unicornio"
written by Rosemary Contreras
illustrated by Victoria Miller

Simon Spotlight/Nickelodeon
New York   London   Toronto   Sydney

Based on the TV series *Dora the Explorer*™ as seen on Nick Jr.™

SIMON SPOTLIGHT
An imprint of Simon & Schuster Children's Publishing Division
1230 Avenue of the Americas, New York, New York 10020
© 2011 Viacom International Inc. All rights reserved. NICKELODEON, NICK JR., *Dora the Explorer*, and all related titles, logos and characters are trademarks of Viacom International Inc.
For information about special discounts for bulk purchases, please contact
Simon & Schuster Special Sales at 1-866-506-1949 or business@simonandschuster.com.
Manufactured in the United States of America 1011 LAK
6 8 10 9 7 5
ISBN 978-1-4424-1312-2

Hi! I am !
DORA

This is !
BOOTS

Do you see a ?
RAINBOW

Look! Someone is coming

down the .
RAINBOW

It is our friend   .
UNICORNIO

Hello,   !
UNICORNIO

Do you see a ?
DOOR

Someone is coming out

of the .
DOOR

It is a .
RABBIT

Hello, !
RABBIT

The  has a
RABBIT

message for .
UNICORNIO

The animals of the
ENCHANTED FOREST

want to be their king.
UNICORNIO

has to go to the

UNICORNIO CASTLE

to get his .

CROWN

Hooray,  !

UNICORNIO

But  UNICORNIO is not sure that he can be a king. He does not think that he is kind, smart, brave, and stro like a king should be.

We can show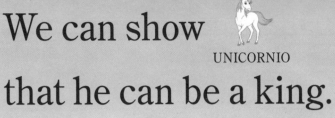
UNICORNIO
that he can be a king.

Will you help?

How do we find the 🏰 ?

CASTLE

says that we need to go

through the .

RIDDLE TREE

Then we need to go

past the .

VOLCANO

Then we will be at the .

CASTLE

On our way to the ,

we see a tiny .

He is too small

to reach the .

Who can help the  ?

ELF

, yeah!

UNICORNIO

is very kind,

UNICORNIO

just like a king should be.

We made it to the  .

RIDDLE TREE

We need to answer

the  's riddle.

RIDDLE TREE

Who can answer the riddle?

, yeah!

UNICORNIO

 is very smart,

UNICORNIO

just like a king should be.

There is the 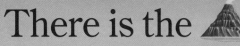.
VOLCANO

There is also a .
DRAGON

Oh, no!

UNICORNIO can create a SHIELD

with his HORN,

but we have to stomp our feet

to make a really big SHIELD.

stomps his feet.

UNICORNIO

 and I stomp our feet.

BOOTS

Will you stomp your feet?

Yeah! We made a big .
SHIELD

It stopped the .
DRAGON

 is very brave,
UNICORNIO

just like a king should be.

We are almost at the 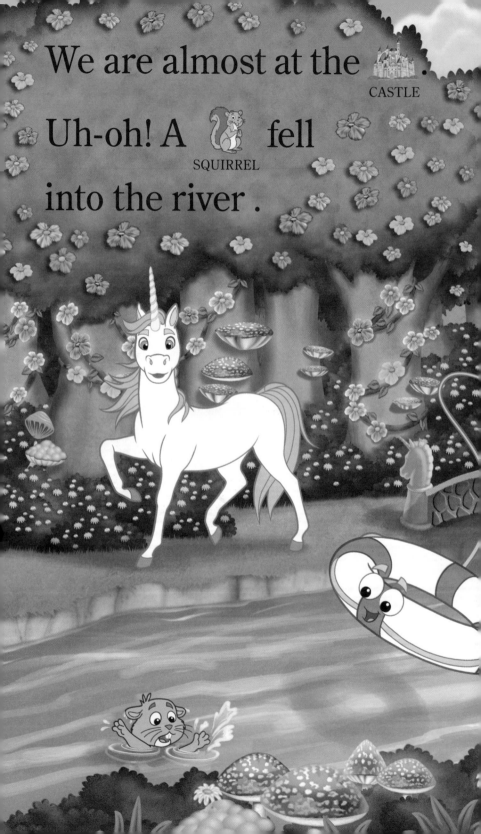 .
CASTLE

Uh-oh! A 🐿 fell
SQUIRREL

into the river .

Someone needs to pull the

SQUIRREL

to safety.

Who can help the ?

 , yeah!

 is very strong,

just like a king should be!

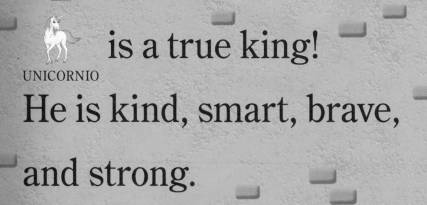

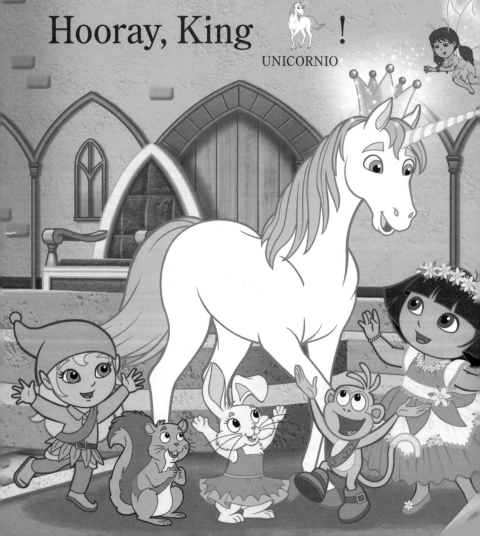 is a true king!

UNICORNIO

He is kind, smart, brave, and strong.

The RABBIT gives UNICORNIO a CROWN.

Hooray, King UNICORNIO!